my best friend

words by julie fogliano

pictures by jillian tamaki

Atheneum Books for Young Readers
NEW YORK LONDON TORONTO SYDNEY NEW DELHI

i have a new friend

and her hair is black
and it shines
and it shines

and she always laughs at everything

she is so smart

and when
i say la la la

she says
la la la

and then we laugh
and turn our hands into ducks
and run away quacking

sometimes when we are feeling quiet
we sit under a big tree

she can turn the leaves
into skeleton hands

she picks away all the green until

BOOO

OOOOOOOOOOOOO

it is a creepy hand
that is chasing me
through the garden

and when i step
on the flowers
she helps me fix them
sort of

if you twirl them
together
they can lean and
look like we never
squashed them

or maybe only a little

she is my best friend
i think

i've never had a best friend
so i'm not sure

but i think she is a really
good best friend

because when we were
drawing

she drew me
and i drew her

and then we made hearts
around it

did you know that when you have
a best friend it is really fun
when you are hiding?

but it is hard not to
make noise

so we sat scrunched
up under the bush
and laughed into
our knees

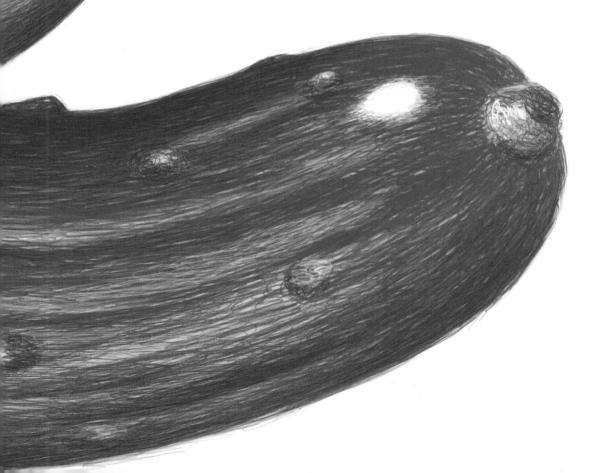

she really likes laughing

she laughed for the whole entire day

especially when
i pretended to be a pickle

she really really liked that

i think i know we are best friends
because

she LOVES
strawberry ice cream

and i HATE
strawberry ice cream

and we are still friends even then

so that
is something good

tomorrow i think we will
write our names

in big letters on the
sidewalk

and it will say
BEST FRIENDS

and there will be a
smiley
and a heart

and my name will
be in red
and her name can
be in green

if green
is what she likes

and i will write mine
in my fanciest writing
and she will write hers
in her own best letters

or maybe her name is

TRFLO

i'm not sure about her name
but i will ask her tomorrow
and she will tell me then

because we are
best friends.

for my sissy, my first best friend.
and for min, who made our charlie's angels complete.—j. f

thank you: JF, the s&s team, SM, MDF, and ST—j. t.

Atheneum

ATHENEUM BOOKS FOR YOUNG READERS • An imprint of Simon & Schuster Children's Publishing Division
1230 Avenue of the Americas, New York, New York 10020 • Text copyright © 2020 by Julie Fogliano • Illustrations
copyright © 2020 by Jillian Tamaki • All rights reserved, including the right of reproduction in whole or in part in
any form. • ATHENEUM BOOKS FOR YOUNG READERS is a registered trademark of Simon & Schuster, Inc. Atheneum logo
is a trademark of Simon & Schuster, Inc. • For information about special discounts for bulk purchases, please contact
Simon & Schuster Special Sales at 1-866-506-1949 or business@simonandschuster.com. • The Simon & Schuster Speakers
Bureau can bring authors to your live event. For more information or to book an event, contact the Simon & Schuster
Speakers Bureau at 1-866-248-3049 or visit our website at www.simonspeakers.com. • Interior design by Ann Bobco and
Michael McCartney • The text for this book was set in Cormorant Garamond. • The illustrations for this book were
digitally rendered. • Manufactured in China • 0821 SCP • 10 9 8 7 6 5 4 3 2 • Library of Congress
Cataloging-in-Publication Data • Names: Fogliano, Julie, author. | Tamaki, Jillian, 1980– illustrator. • Title: My best
friend / Julie Fogliano ; illustrated by Jillian Tamaki. • Description: First edition. | New York : Atheneum, [2020] | Summary:
Two girls quickly become best friends, even before they learn one another's names. • Identifiers: LCCN 2018039466
ISBN 9781534427228 (hardcover) | ISBN 9781534427235 (eBook) • Subjects: | CYAC: Best friends—Fiction. | Friendship—Fiction.
Classification: LCC PZ7.F6763 My 2020 (print) | DDC [E]—dc23 • LC record available at https://lccn.loc.gov/2018039466